Betsy Byars

ME TARZAN

Illustrations by Bill Cigliano

SCHOLASTIC INC.

New York Toronto London Auckland Sydney
Mexico City New Delhi Hong Kong

For Angela

ISBN 0-439-30468-7

12 11 10 9 8 7 6 5 4 3 2 1   1 2 3 4 5 6/0

Printed in the U.S.A.   40

First Scholastic printing, September 2001

Typography by Al Cetta

Contents

One / Being Tarzan

Dorothy threw open the kitchen door.

AHHHHHH-AHH-AHH-AHHHH AHH-AHH-AHH-AHHHHHHHHHHHHH

Her mother rushed into the kitchen. "What was that?"

"Me, Mom! I got it!"

"What?"

"Tarzan! I'm going to be Tarzan in the play."

"Why Tarzan? Weren't there any parts for girls?"

"Yes, but here's what happened: I was sitting there, trying to decide what to be, when Dwayne Wiggert got up. He goes, 'I want to try out for Tarzan.' And Mom, he gives this pitiful yell—ah—ah—ah, like he was at the doctor's office. Oh, I forgot to tell you that Dwayne Wiggert is my enemy."

"I wasn't aware you'd been at this school long enough to get an enemy."

"I got him the first day. I had on my purple outfit and he says, "I didn't know anybody had legs like that except Barney."

Her mother said, "There is nothing wrong with your legs."

"Mom, they barely reach the ground. Anyway, I decided to get revenge. I put up my hand. Mr. Mooney goes, 'What part are you going to try out for, Dorothy?' I say, 'Same as him.'

""Tarzan?" he asked. He sounded like you, Mom, as if there's something wrong with a girl wanting to be Tarzan.

"I said, 'Yes, Sir, Tarzan.' The class snickered, and so Mr. Mooney very quickly added, 'Now, gang, a girl can be Tarzan these days.' He does not want to be accused of being sexist."

Her mother sighed.

"I got up and turned around to face the class, and, and—I don't even know if I can explain what happened."

"Try."

"Well, I felt this huge power come over me. It was awesome. I could smell the jungle and the apes—

though to be honest, that might have been Howie Sanders, who sits in the front row and doesn't take baths.

"It was like I knew the jungle. I felt the wildness, the primitive emotions—"

"Don't exaggerate, Dottie."

"I'm not. And in the middle of all this, I opened my mouth and inhaled the jungle and out came something that even the real Tarzan would have envied. Want to hear it?"

"I just did. I—"

"Actually, when the urge hits me, I can't stop myself. It's coming over me now."

Dorothy threw back her head. Her hands rose to her chest.

AHHHHHH-AHH-AHH-AAHH-AHHHHH-

AHH-AHH-AHH-AHHHHHHHHHHHHHHHHH

Her mother stepped back, stunned. She put one hand to her head as if something inside had been jarred loose. "It's getting louder."

"I know—every time I do it," Dorothy said proudly.

"And Mom, after I did it in class, there was this silence, and then guess what?"

"I can't."

"We heard this creaking, and it was Clampster."

"Who?"

"Clampster, the class hamster. For weeks we've been trying to get him on his exercise wheel and he would not get on, and all of a sudden, guess what?"

"He gets on."

"Mom, how did you know? And he's not just on, he's going a hundred miles an hour."

While she was talking, a dog across the street howled to be let out and a stray cat climbed the tree beside the kitchen window to peer inside.

"And then the principal came. He said, 'Everything all right in here?'

"Mr. Mooney said, 'I hope we didn't disturb you. We're having auditions for our literary play.'

"'Maybe you should hold these after school.'

"Mr. Mooney said, 'Auditions for the part of Tarzan are now over, so things should calm down.' The principal left, and Mr. Mooney turned to the class.

"He lifted his hands as if he were helpless, caught in a force greater than himself—like I am." Dorothy grinned. "Then he said, 'Dorothy will be our Tarzan.'

"'Thank you,' I said. I went back to my seat. Dwayne put his foot out in the aisle to trip me, but hey, a foot is not going to stop Tarzan. No way. I stepped over it and sat down.

"It was the best I have felt since we moved here. I felt so good I sent Dwayne a note—four words. Guess what they were?"

"I can't."

Dorothy grinned.

"Me Tarzan, you Dwayne."

Two / Me Dwayne

"What's wrong, Dwayne?"

"Nothing!"

"Did something happen at school?"

"No!"

Dwayne went into his room and slammed the door, a sure sign that something had happened at school.

His mother stopped at the closed door. She heard his schoolbooks being thrown on the floor, his body being thrown on the bed.

"Dwayne—"

"Nothing's wrong!"

"I made cookies. They're for school, but you—"

"I'm not hungry."

"They're in the shape of stars—you know, in honor of the play. Speaking of the play, this was the big day, wasn't it? Did you try out?"

"Yes, I tried out." His tone was flat, the tone his father used when he lost an important sale.

"Did you get Tarzan?"

"No, I did not get Tarzan."

"But your yell was great. You sounded just like Carol Burnett."

"I wanted to sound like Tarzan."

"Who got it?"

"Some girl."

"A girl Tarzan?"

"Yes!

"Well, that is carrying women's lib way too far. Next thing you know a woman will want to be—" She broke off, unable to think of anything women didn't want to be. Finally she came up with "Pope!" but she wasn't even sure of that.

Dwayne heard his mother's footsteps retreat down the hall. He opened his eyes and saw his cat, Wiggie. His expression eased.

He said, "Wiggie, you are the only person in this world I can talk to, the only person who understands."

Wiggie was sitting on Dwayne's desk, pretending he wasn't interested in the contents of the tropical fish tank.

"Wiggie, there's this new girl in my school named Dorothy." He took in a deep breath. "On her first day, I was looking at her in the cafeteria. Don't ask me why.

"So she looks up and sees me looking at her. I immediately look away, of course, but a minute later I look back to see if she's looking to see if I'm looking, and while I'm looking she looks and sees me. Again!

"And it keeps going on and on like that. I can't help myself. I have to look and see if she's looking. By the end of lunch, with all the looking, I haven't had anything to eat.

"I am leaving the cafeteria, tired and hungry, and this girl and I meet in the doorway. Actually we bump into each other. I can see that she thinks I planned it. She thinks I've been looking at her all through lunch because I like her and that I deliberately planned to bump into her. So I said something I heard someone say on TV: 'I didn't know anybody had legs like that except Barney.' Don't ask me why I said it. Actually I hadn't even seen her legs—they were under the table while I was staring. Later I did look, and her legs were all right.

"So, in case you're wondering why I'm lying on this bed without the part of Tarzan, that's how it started."

Three / Almost Like an Elephant

"Dad, want to hear me do Tarzan?" Dorothy asked.

"Will it take long? Jeff's picking me up for bowling."

"One minute—max."

"I can spare a minute." Her father stopped. He was holding his bowling ball at the end of one arm as if ready to roll it.

Dorothy stepped back a few steps. "I don't want to blow you away."

"I can take it," he said mildly.

Dorothy threw back her head. Again she seemed to smell the jungle. She felt power, a primitive power. It was such a strong sensation that it made her feel she was not only in the jungle, she was master of it.

She wished she had a vine so she could swing across the living room. She glanced up at the light fixture, dangling on its cord. Better not. Her hands at her sides were fists. She felt like beating them against her chest. Better not.

She opened her mouth.

AHHHHHH-AHH-AHH-AHH-AHHHHHHHHHHHHHHH-AHH-AHH-AHH-AHHHHHH

Her father dropped his bowling ball with a thud.

Her mother rushed in from the kitchen, one hand holding her head again.

"Dorothy, I asked you not to do that."

"Dad wanted to hear my yell. And oh, Dad, guess what? I got the part of Tarzan over Dwayne Wiggert. His yell was not half as loud as mine."

"I don't doubt that."

"So. What did you think?"

"Where are you going to do this, er, yell?" he asked in a careful way.

"Onstage. At school. For the PTA. You and mom will get to hear it."

"Ah."

Her dad retrieved his bowling ball and put it in

the carrying case with his shoes.

The stray cat had moved from the kitchen window to where the action was—the living-room window. It had been joined by two dogs, who moved uneasily beneath the tree and into the shrubbery, looking for something they had not until this moment known existed.

A car horn sounded outside. "There's my ride." Her dad opened the front door. "Get away from here! What are all these animals doing in our yard? Isn't there a leash law?"

"Not for cats, Dad."

"Well, at least two of these are dogs, and one of them looks like a rottweiler."

Dorothy stood behind her father in the open doorway. "I wonder what they want."

"Get away from here!" her father yelled.

He began making his way down the walk to the waiting car. He glanced over his shoulder at Dorothy.

"Don't let these animals into the house. Shoo, scram, get away from here, scat, go home."

Dorothy started to close the door, but she paused to listen. A coonhound bayed from some distant farm. And then—and then there was a trumpeting sound, almost like an elephant.

The dogs and cats were looking at Dorothy, waiting. She showed them her empty hands. "I don't have anything. Go home."

She closed the door. "My imagination is running away with me," she said.

"Did you say something to me?" her mother called from the kitchen.

"I was talking to myself, but you won't believe this. I heard something that sounded like an elephant."

"I didn't know there was anything that sounded like an elephant," her mom called back, "except an elephant."

"That's what I was thinking."

As she climbed the stairs to her room, she had a premonition of something in her future. She couldn't see exactly what it was, but the thought left her excited and yet somehow afraid.

Four / Wiggie

It was after supper. Dwayne was continuing his chat with Wiggie, but Wiggie wouldn't look at him. That was all right. If Dwayne only had conversations with people who looked at him, he would only talk to TV news anchors.

"In case you're wondering," he told the cat, "here's how I lost Tarzan."

The cat blinked but didn't yawn, so Dwayne figured Wiggie might be interested.

Dwayne loved this cat. The cat had followed him home one day, and after a humiliating period of begging his mom—he had promised everything from perfect behavior to perfect grades—he had been allowed to keep Wiggie.

"But if those grades don't pick up . . ." his mother

had warned, pointing dramatically from the cat to the door.

Well, his grades had picked up. Fortunately she hadn't said his grades had to stay up.

Since that first day Wiggie had pretended to believe that no life existed outside the walls of this house. It was as if his life on the streets hadn't been anything to write home about, and if he went out, he might not get back in.

"This girl I was telling you about, well, she must have been very angry about what I said about her legs, because today she took revenge.

"You, of all people, know how hard I've been practicing my Tarzan yell. You've heard me—well, you would have heard me if you hadn't run out of the room every time I started it."

"Anyway, I was good, even if I do say so myself. So I got up in front of the class to audition, and I gave a perfect yell. I was proud of it. Then Dorothy got up."

Dwayne looked at the cat to see if he understood the significance of the word Dorothy. Wiggie yawned.

Sometimes it seemed to Dwayne that the cat was just about to say something, something in human talk. This was one of those moments. And Dwayne was afraid he knew what the cat would say: "Bor-ring."

"Well," he said as if in self-defense, "if you had heard her Tarzan yell, you wouldn't be bored."

Suddenly, as if on cue, as if he had actually heard the yell, Wiggie lifted his head.

"What's wrong?" Dwayne asked.

Wiggie's yellow eyes had a wild jungle look that Dwayne had never seen before. Even when they took him to the vet, he didn't look this wild.

Dwayne put out one hand to scratch Wiggie behind the ears, but Wiggie jumped down and ran into the kitchen. Dwayne followed.

"What's gotten into the cat?" his mom asked from the sink.

"I don't know, Mom. He was sitting there, yawning, and then all of a sudden he got this wild look in his eyes." He picked up the cat, who did not want to be picked up.

"You are not going out," he told him. "You've forgotten what it's like. It's a jungle out there."

Five / The Jungle Out There

Dorothy lay in the dark, her eyes closed. She was breathing as slowly as possible.

Tonight was like the eve of something—Christmas or New Year's. Something big was about to happen.

She felt the Tarzan yell rising within her. It was as if the yell couldn't wait until tomorrow. She told herself, "No! Mom and Dad are in bed down the hall, and they have made it very clear they don't want to hear another Tarzan yell."

Dorothy raised up on one elbow and took a deep breath. She threw back the covers.

Silently she got out of bed and crossed the room to the window. Moonlight laced the yard.

She opened the window. She could hear the locusts, the tree frogs. She took a deep breath to push the yell deeper inside her. Instead, the fresh air brought with it the primal scent of the forest.

She moved to the chair where she had dropped her clothes. Silently she pulled on her jeans and tucked her nightshirt inside.

She tiptoed down the carpeted stairs and went through the dark kitchen and out the back door.

In the moonlight the yard was no longer familiar. The swings, left by the former owners, blew back and forth in the breeze, creating strange, alien shadows on the lawn.

She walked across the grass, barely feeling the blades beneath her feet. She continued into the grove of trees behind the garage.

There she stopped. She heard a new sound—a wild, rhythmic beating. Native drums? The throbbing of her own heart? She couldn't be sure of anything tonight.

A hoot owl called in the woods, and it seemed to speak directly to her. She tried to shake off the feeling that she was somewhere other than her own back-yard.

She glanced around. There were other houses in the neighborhood, but they were hidden by the thickness of the trees. She might disturb the neighborhood, she reminded herself. Windows would be thrown open all up and down the street. Someone would call the police. Her parents would—

She smiled. Oh, one Tarzan yell couldn't hurt anyone. It would be over in a minute. Anyway, there was no stopping it now.

Beneath her feet was not grass—it was dead and decaying vegetation. As her feet shifted, the rich scent of it filled her nostrils.

The shrubbery was not azaleas and jasmine, but giant creepers and elephant-ear fern. The trees beyond were not maple and cottonwood, but primeval forest.

Now the Tarzan yell was rising within her. She couldn't have stopped it if she tried. She threw back her head.

AHHHHHHH-AHH-AHH-AHH-AHHHHHH-AHH-AHH-AHH-AHHHHHHH

She did not move for a moment, and then she sighed with satisfaction. It was so—yes, satisfying was the only word to describe it. She wondered why everybody in the world wasn't standing out under the stars, throwing back their heads and—

Suddenly she heard a noise.

She held her breath.

The noise came again. Someone, something—was at the fence.

The sound was closer. Someone, something—was in the trees, leaping among the branches.

It couldn't be an ape—not here in the Forestwood Downs section of town—but it was something big that traveled through the trees.

The final crash was directly overhead. Leaves rained down on Dorothy's head. She stepped back and looked up.

At that moment a dark cloud swirled in front of the moon, and she stood in darkness. She waited, her eyes lifted to the limb of the cottonwood tree.

There was silence now, as if whatever was overhead were waiting too. Then the cloud passed, and the full moon lit up the night.

Above her, on a low-hanging branch, was a majestic body, dark and sleek. And gleaming in the moonlight were golden eyes.

Dorothy could not move. She was frozen in place. Then there was a new sound—not a roar but a sort of purring.

Dorothy didn't wait to hear any more. She turned and ran as hard as she could for the house.

As she ran, the noises of the jungle began to recede, replaced by the sounds of civilization. A car honked in the street, a plane arched across the sky, an audience laughed on a neighbor's television.

And behind her, from the low-hanging branches of the cottonwood tree, the slanted golden eyes watched where she went.

Six / Gotcha!

Dwayne lay in the dark, staring up at the ceiling.

This had been the worst day of his life. Not only had he lost the part of Tarzan, but after supper his mother had let Wiggie out. Wiggie! The only person in the world who understood him!

Dwayne had gone into the kitchen to feed Wiggie, and his mother had looked up apologetically. "Wiggie got out."

"What?"

"I opened the door to take out the garbage. While the door was open, the fool cat comes streaking into the room, runs between my feet, and escapes."

"Mom! I asked you to be careful!"

"The cat will come back. Cats always come back. They have a natural instinct."

Now two hours had passed and Wiggie had not come home.

Dwayne got out of bed. He pulled on his jeans over his pajamas. He walked soundlessly through the kitchen and out the back door.

"Here, Wiggie, kitty, kitty," he called softly. No answer.

He moved to the street and turned in the direction of the park. Now he was far enough away from the house to call louder. "Wiggie! Wiggie!" No answer.

He turned down Oak Street and moved toward Forestwood Downs. It was here that Dwayne had found the cat, so perhaps Wiggie had gone this way.

Dwayne walked slowly along the darkened sidewalk, ducking into the shadows when an occasional car passed.

"Wiggie! Wiggie!"

He paused at a bend in the road. Ahead, he could see animals had gathered in one of the yards. Dogs and cats—lots of them. Maybe some animal was in heat, maybe many animals. He broke into a run.

As he got closer to the house, he paused. "Wiggie!" His eyes searched the pack of restless animals. There he was! "Wiggie!"

Wiggie turned and gave Dwayne a wild-eyed look, as if he'd never seen Dwayne before in his life and didn't want to see him again. Then Wiggie ran into the shrubbery.

In the moonlight Dwayne could see Wiggie's tail snapping from side to side as if he were irritated. Then he disappeared around the corner of the house. Keeping close to the shrubbery, Dwayne moved after him.

At that moment the back door of the house opened, and a figure—a girl's—stepped out into the moonlight. As she glanced up, the moonlight fell on her face.

Dwayne drew in his breath. It was her! Dorothy!

What was she doing out here? Dwayne had a reason to be out at night—he was looking for his lost cat. But what reason could she have for coming outside?

He wanted to follow her directly into the trees, but instead he moved to the fence and made his way in the shadows.

Her footsteps stopped. His did too. She was so still, she didn't even seem to be breathing. He wasn't breathing either. It was as if the whole world were waiting for something. Then it came.

AHH-AHH-AHH-AHH-AHHHHHH-

AHH-AHH-AHH-AHHHHHHHHHHHHH!

He stepped back against the fence, stunned by what he had heard. It was even louder than it had been at school.

There was a long pause, and then something dark came over the fence, an animal, but unlike any animal Dwayne had seen before. Some kind of lion? An ape? Dwayne didn't care for either one of them.

Then there was silence, and Dwayne leaned forward. He heard something—a sort of deep purring, too loud for a cat and yet—

At that moment Dorothy came running out from among the trees, as if whatever was in the trees were after her. Dwayne drew back, but he felt he could have stepped right in her path and she wouldn't have noticed.

She ran into the house and slammed the door behind her.

Dwayne glanced down. Wiggie came out of the bushes, his ears back, his tail wide as a plume, running for the action at the grove of trees.

Dwayne scooped him up.

"Gotcha!" he said, and then, heart racing, he, like Dorothy, ran as hard as he could for home.

Seven / Puma

"Did you read this story about the circus?" Dorothy's mother asked at the breakfast table.

Her father said, "Pass me the sports section."

"It turns out that the circus is already in town. Two performances in Florida were canceled because of the brush fires. They're going to be here for three days."

Dorothy's mom liked to read stories from the morning paper. She especially liked animal stories— dogs saving their masters, cats walking a hundred miles to be with their families, iguanas setting off fire alarms in school labs.

"The story says the animals were disturbed last night. Maybe that *was* an elephant you heard."

"Disturbed?" Dorothy asked quickly. She had been sitting quietly, moving her cereal around as if she were eating.

"It says that last night when the keeper was making his eight-o'clock rounds, the elephants—"

"Eight o'clock?" That had been about the time she'd stood in the living room and given the Tarzan yell for her dad.

"Is anything wrong, Dottie?" her mother asked.

"No."

"Are you coming down with something?"

"I just didn't sleep much last night. Go on about the animals. Did anything else happen, like, later in the evening?"

"How did you know? Yes! The circus owns a puma. It's young, and the trainer says it doesn't perform yet. The puma escaped her cage sometime between eleven and twelve."

"Puma? Big cat?" Dorothy's voice wavered.

"Yes. I hope it doesn't come here. It's not that far through the woods, you know, to the circus grounds."

"Let me read it."

Her mother folded the paper and put it firmly beside her plate. "You do not have time to waste on the morning paper," she told Dorothy. "And you don't either," she told Dorothy's father. "You should have left for the office ten minutes ago."

"I'm outta here," he said.

Mom turned back to Dorothy. "And you're going to miss your bus."

"Is there a picture of the puma?"

"No. What they're afraid is going to happen—and what probably will happen—is that some gun-happy man is going to shoot it. Here comes your bus. Go."

Dorothy left the kitchen and picked up her books. Then she set them down again and, after a moment, went slowly back into the kitchen.

"You've missed your bus."

"I know."

"Well, I'm not going to make a habit of driving you to school."

"I know. Mom—"

"You're sick. I knew you were sick. I—"

"I saw the puma."

"Now I know you're sick."

"Mom, just listen to me. I went out in the yard last night after everyone was asleep. Now don't start yelling at me, just listen."

"I'm listening, but get on with it."

"I went back to the trees and gave my Tarzan yell. I couldn't help myself. Afterward I stood there, and I don't know how much time passed. It was like I was in a trance. Nothing smelled the way our yard smells, and none of the noises were our neighborhood noises.

"Then I heard crashing, like something was leaping through the trees.

"The moon went behind a cloud, and when it came out, Mom, I saw a huge creature on a low branch."

Her mother gave Dorothy a hard, searching look. "You really think you saw this, don't you?"

Dorothy nodded.

"Show me."

Dorothy and her mother walked across the yard to the trees. It seemed impossible now, in broad daylight.

"The only reason I am coming out here in the yard in my bathrobe—well, it's like I used to come into your room when you thought something was under your bed. I knew nothing was under your bed, but the only way to satisfy you that nothing was under your bed was to get down on my hands and knees and look and say, 'Nothing is under—'"

"There."

"Where?"

Suddenly her mother took a breath so deep, it used up almost all the air in the neighborhood.

"Puma!" she cried.

"I know, Mom."

"Puma!"

"Be quiet or you'll scare it away."

"Puma! Puma!"

Her mother turned and started for the house. Then, remembering she had left her daughter, she ran back and grabbed Dorothy's arm.

"Don't you know what that is?" she cried.

"Yes, Mom, it's a—"

"Puma!" her mother interrupted, and dragging Dorothy along, she ran for the house.

"See, Dwayne, I told you the cat would come back."

"Mom, the cat did not come back. I went out and got him."

"When?"

"Last night." Dwayne changed the subject quickly. "Now don't let the cat out while I'm at school."

"I'll try not to, but—" She broke off. "Where are you going?"

"School."

"The bus won't be here for thirty minutes. Sit down and have some breakfast. I've never known you to be in such a hurry to get to school."

"I'm not in a hurry," he said defensively.

But Dwayne had been in a hurry to get to school ever since he'd gotten home with Wiggie last night. And that had been about twelve o'clock. So since midnight, for the first time in his life, he had been in a hurry to go to school.

He had done something else for the first time in his life: written a note to a girl. He had worked on the note all night in his mind, and when he had gotten up this morning, he had put it on paper. It was perfect— humorous and yet mysterious.

What was that last night? One of your apes?

"Good morning, class."

"Good morning, Mr. Mooney."

Dwayne was the only one who didn't join in the greeting. He was busy wondering where Dorothy was.

Her desk was empty. And as he stared at it, the empty desk seemed to take on a sort of deeper meaning, like the riderless horse at a cowboy's funeral, a plane missing from a formation at a funeral for a pilot, an empty space that—

"Dwayne? Dwayne!"

Dwayne focused his eyes on the teacher. "Yes, Mr. Mooney?"

Because of the importance of the matter, Mr. Mooney decided to speak to the whole class this time.

"Class, what are these things on the side of your heads?"

Mr. Mooney couldn't stump them on this. "Ears!"

"And what do you do with ears?"

"Listen!"

"And how does it make your teacher feel when he sees that you are not using these ears?"

They didn't get to yell, "Mad!" because the door opened. It was Dorothy.

Mr. Mooney said, "Welcome to *The Twilight Zone*, Dorothy."

"I'm sorry I'm late, Mr. Mooney."

"I am too, but you haven't missed much. Class, take out your journals."

Dorothy sat in her desk. She had her journal out before anybody else. She didn't even pause to think but bent forward with intensity. She wrote.

Dwayne took the note out of his pocket and passed it to her. His eyes gleamed with anticipation.

She glanced at the note and stuffed it in the back of her journal. Had she even read it? What kind of girl would just stuff an important note in the back of her journal? He knew the answer.

Dorothy!

Dorothy!

D·o·r·o·t·h·y!

King of the jungle.

nine / D·O·R·O·T·H·Y

Last night was the weirdest night of my life,

Dorothy wrote.

I went outside to do my Tarzan yell.

It was the best Tarzan yell I have ever, ever done—maybe that anybody has ever, ever done—and after I did it, I heard crashing and a huge animal landed in the tree overhead.

Its eyes were golden and it was looking right at me—like: I'm here, what are you going to do now? What I was going to do was run into the house.

This morning Mom read in the paper that a puma was missing from the circus. Mom was worried that someone might shoot the puma, and so for the good of the puma, I had to tell her it was in our backyard.

Mom called the newspaper, and a reporter came out with the animal trainer.

Mom was saying things to me like "Now don't mention about your being out in the middle of the night. Now don't mention anything about Tarzan. And whatever you do, don't do that awful yell."

The trainer and the reporter came, and the trainer got the puma back into his cage. Then the reporter took some pictures of me and the puma.

The puma kept looking at me as if he were waiting for something, and the trouble was that I knew what he was waiting for, but I couldn't help him.

On the way to school my mom asked me to promise something. I hate this because she makes me promise before I know the promise.

"I understand that you have to give your yell in the play, but I'm beginning to think that—"

"Showtime!" Mr. Mooney said. He pushed his chair back from his desk and stood.

Dwayne glanced at Dorothy's desk. She was still working on her journal.

"—I'm beginning to think that this yell of yours means something to animals, that it's somehow the call of the wild. . . ."

"Dorothy, do you plan to join us?" Mr. Mooney asked.

Dorothy looked up, startled. She put one hand up to her face as if to adjust her glasses, which she didn't wear. "Sure."

Ten / Tarzan's Turn

Dorothy rose, closed her journal, and set it under her desk. Then, in the same careful way, she walked to the front of the room. Dwayne thought it was as if she'd been put together by unskilled labor.

"Mr. Mooney?"

Mr. Mooney was busy handing out the scripts. He said, "Yes," without turning to see who had spoken.

"Mr. Mooney," Dorothy went on, her voice so low Dwayne would have missed it entirely if he had not gotten up out of his seat on the pretense of being eager to get his script.

"Yes, Dorothy, what is it?"

"Mr. Mooney, I have a little problem."

"You're lucky it's just a little problem. I have a big problem. Some of these scripts are missing."

"We can share," Clarissa said helpfully. She was the moderator and eager to get on with it.

"Good, Clarissa. Gang, we'll have to share today, but tomorrow everyone will have his or her own personal script. Now, oh, yes, Dorothy, what is your problem?"

"I was wondering if—just for today—I could *say* my Tarzan yell instead of, you know, giving it my all."

"Yes. Actually, gang, it's usual in the theater that on the first rehearsal, the cast simply reads through the script, not trying to, as Dorothy put it, give it their all. This will be a read-through."

He glanced around. "Clarissa, this is your big moment. Are you ready?"

"Yes."

Clarissa began with a loud, "Welcome to our show. Mr. Herb Mooney's class is proud to present a revue of famous characters from the books we have come to love."

Clarissa turned to smile apologetically at Mr. Mooney. "I can't help it if I act a little bit, Mr. Mooney. I just love this play."

"Feel free, Clarissa. You're setting the stage very well."

"Thank you." Clarissa got her stage voice back. "Through history there have been characters that seem to walk off the page. Why, here comes one now."

There was an awkward pause, and then Clarissa said, "That's you, Dwayne. Come on, get with it. That's you."

As Dwayne stepped forward, Dorothy began to tremble.

She had suddenly remembered Dwayne's note. She hadn't paid much attention to it when he had given it to her. She had been in a rush to write in her journal. Now the words came back with such force, it took her breath away.

What was that last night? One of your apes?

Dwayne Wiggart had been in her yard last night! He had seen her sneak out of the house! He had heard her yell! He, of all people, had—

"I'm nervous too," Emma Lou said sympathetically.

Dorothy and Emma Lou were sharing a script, and Dorothy's half was trembling so hard, Emma Lou said, "Here, let me hold it."

"Thanks."

Emma Lou began doing all the work now, turning the pages, holding the place with her finger. She whispered, "Oh, Mary Poppins is next. That's me."

She stepped forward and said brightly, "With this umbrella I can fly over town, and remember? A spoonful of sugar makes the medicine go down."

She paused, gave Mr. Mooney an anxious look, and then said in her regular voice, "Was that all right, Mr. Mooney?"

"Fine. Remember you'll need an umbrella. Gang, we're going to try to keep the props to a minimum, but if the prop is mentioned in your verse, then you'll need to have it. Yes, Carl?"

"Where am I going to get a hook for my arm? Remember, I'm Captain Hook."

"We'll work on that, Carl."

"He could make one out of a coat hanger," Clarissa said. "My brother did that one Halloween."

"There you go," Mr. Mooney said. "Now, where were we?"

"I had just said my part, Mr. Mooney. With this umbrella I fly all over town, and remember? A spoonful of sugar makes the medicine go down." Emma Lou stepped back.

"Clarissa?"

Clarissa looked down at her script. "Some characters on the pages we have found can be known just by their sound."

There was a silence. Mr. Mooney checked his own script.

"Tarzan! Tarzan?"

Emma Lou's finger found the place on the page. "That's you."

Dorothy cleared her throat. She reminded herself that she was going to *read* her Tarzan yell.

"Anything wrong, Tarzan?" Mr. Mooney said.

Yes! She was beginning to smell the jungle and feel the lush tropical vines. She heard the animals. The Tarzan yell was in her very soul, waiting to explode.

"Give her the lead-in again."

Clarissa said, "Some characters on the pages we have found can be known just by their sound."

"The yell, the yell," Mr. Mooney said. "Let's hear the yell. You've got to be quick on the yell, Tarzan, or it won't be funny. Timing is everything. Give her the lead-in again."

Clarissa read in a flat, singsong voice this time as if to show that three lead-ins were too many for anybody. "Some characters on the pages we have found can be known just by their sound."

Mr. Mooney began humming the theme song from *Jeopardy!*, always a sign of great impatience.

Dorothy took in a deep breath and threw back her head.

AHHHHHHH-AHH-AHH'
AAHH-AHHHHH-AHH-AHH
AHH-AHHHHHHH

Dorothy felt wonderful, fulfilled. There was something so satisfying about the yell; it was as if it reminded—not just animals, but people as well—that once they had been wild and free.

Her thoughts stopped as she realized the class had gone quiet. The only sound was that of Clampster exceeding the speed limit.

She glanced around. None of her classmates seemed to have been reminded that once they had been wild and free. In fact they needed to be reminded to close their mouths.

It was Mr. Mooney who managed to think of something to say.

"Well, Dorothy, if that was not 'giving it your all,' as you put it, I'll have to get earplugs for when you do."

Eleven / APB

Mr. Mooney was saying, "You should all have your props tomorrow. We'll have a dress rehearsal in the auditorium at—"

He was interrupted by the loudspeaker.

"Not another All Points Bulletin," Mr. Mooney sighed. "Listen up, gang."

"This is the principal's office. Mrs. Hutchinson has requested that all students remain in their present rooms until they are excused."

Everyone in the class looked around for an explanation. Mr. Mooney lifted his hands in a gesture that said he didn't understand either.

"The school yard is at present filled with animals—dogs and cats as well as seven horses from the Friendly City Riding Academy. The owners of the horses are on their way and will need time to catch the horses and ride them back to the academy.

"When the horses are out of the school yard, Mrs. Hutchinson will allow those students who can identify their dogs and cats to go out, leash them, and take them home. Apparently there is also an iguana.

"Thank you for your attention."

43

"You're late, Dottie."

"I know, Mom. There were some horses in the school yard, and we couldn't go out until they were caught."

"Horses! Pumas! What next?"

"That's what I'm wondering." Dorothy stood tiredly in the doorway, her book bag sagging on one arm.

"Well, this will cheer you up. I was on TV! The noon news!"

"What?" Dorothy asked blankly.

She was still upset about what had happened at the rehearsal. It seemed to her that after that awesome

AHHHHHH-AHH-AHH-AHH-

AHHHHH-AHH-AHH-AHH-AHHHHHHHHHHHHHH

everyone in the class—including Mr. Mooney—had been avoiding her. It was as if they were afraid that if they came too close, they would catch her weirdness.

"I was on the noon news. I taped it. Don't you remember the puma?"

"Oh, that."

Dorothy started for her room.

Her mother followed her into the hall and passed her. "Don't you want to see the tape?"

"Maybe later."

"There's even a shot of the puma back in his cage at the circus. He's not doing much—just lying there, looking sad, as if he's missed his big chance in life.

"In the interview I give you complete credit."

Her mother followed Dorothy to the door of her

45

room, re-creating her interview.

"I said, 'My daughter noticed the young puma, and she and I called the newspaper—we didn't have the phone number of the circus.'

"I said some more, but they cut it out. Anyway, guess what? We're going to be guests of the circus on Friday night.

"I can't wait," her mother said, hugging herself. "I have not been to the circus in years. I'd forgotten how much fun it used to be. Of course, now you see wild animals every day on TV, but it's not the same as going to the circus."

"I can't go on Friday," Dorothy said bluntly.

"But why?"

"Friday's the night of the PTA play." Suddenly Dorothy's face brightened. "Though maybe Mr. Mooney will excuse me to go to the circus. I could ask."

"No, I want you to be in the play."

"The rehearsal didn't go very well."

"You know what they say—bad rehearsal, great performance."

"I wish."

"I'm going to send tapes of the interview to everyone back home. I am so proud of you."

Dorothy thought once again of the feeling that had come over her at the rehearsal, of the uncontrollable urge to do the Tarzan yell, of the yell that had been so loud, she had startled even herself.

"I hope you always will be," she said.

Thirteen / What If . . .

Mr. Mooney let out a sigh of relief. At last the classroom was empty. The school building was quiet.

The horses were back in their stable. The cats and dogs had been leashed and led reluctantly away. The school buses had rolled to the suburbs. He didn't know what had happened to the iguana, the boa constrictor, and the parrot that kept saying, "Hello, Cookie," and he didn't care.

Quiet . . . peace . . . bliss . . .

Mr. Mooney looked around the room, and his eyes focused on a single desk—Dorothy's.

The girl interested him. It wasn't just that she had the vocal cords of a bull elephant; it was the expressions that came over her face.

He recalled the rehearsal. Just before Dorothy's yell, she had appeared reluctant, uncertain, almost as if she would rather have been anywhere else in the world.

And then came that unbelievable

AHHHHH-AHH-AHH-AAHH-AHHHHH-AHH-AHH-AHH-AHHHHHHHHHHHHHHH!

It had actually made the hair stand up on the back of his neck, the way an animal's hackles rise. He had not even been aware he had hair on his neck, but he obviously had. He rubbed his neck thoughtfully.

Then after the yell, he recalled, her face had had a joyous look, as if she had been set free in some way.

Mr. Mooney leaned forward. The key to the girl and what she was thinking was in her journal. Mr. Mooney had told the class when he passed out the journals that what they wrote was strictly private.

"Except from you," someone at the back of the room had sneered.

"No, these are your journals, and I respect your privacy."

Mr. Mooney got up. He moved down the row of desks, uneven now because of the rush to exit. He paused at Dorothy's desk, remembering that while all the other students had been at the windows, trying to see the stray horses and animals, Dorothy had sat at her desk, bent over her journal.

Sometimes, he reminded himself, a teacher must—for the good of the individual student—break his word.

He found that this freed his conscience, as it usually did, and he knelt by Dorothy's desk. The journal was on top, and he took it out and read.

Tomorrow is Thursday, the dress rehearsal for our play.

Once again I will give my Tarzan yell. Here's what has happened so far.

Yell for tryout: Clampster ran around his cage.

Yells for Mom: Dogs and cats came to my house.

Yell for Dad: More dogs and cats came, a coonhound bayed, and an elephant trumpeted.

Yell in backyard: A puma escaped the circus and came looking for me.

Yell for rehearsal: Horses escaped from the Friendly City Riding Academy and came to the school, along with dogs and cats and an iguana.

I don't know what will happen tomorrow, but I have decided that I am not going to be afraid about what people think. I'm just going to give it my all. If animals come, let them. It seems to me that animals are missing something in their tame lives, something they are aware their ancestors had, and my yell helps them remember.

What if . . .

Mr. Mooney closed Dorothy's journal. She hadn't finished that last sentence.

Yes, what if . . .

He recalled this afternoon, when he had joined the principal in the school yard and stared at the horses, dogs, and cats. He recalled her angry "I mean to find out who's responsible for this."

"There probably isn't any one person," he'd said. "It's probably a—a freak accident. Horses run away from the stable, and dogs and cats catch their panic and start running too."

"No, there's something more here."

He had been saved from further discussion with the principal by the arrival of the Friendly City Riding Academy girls.

And now Mr. Mooney finished that terrible sentence that began with "What if . . ."

"What if I get fired?"

Fourteen / Onstage

"Before we go to the auditorium, gang, I want to make a few changes in the script."

"Don't change me—I've already got my hook." Carl lifted his coat hanger in a menacing way.

"No, Carl, you're fine." A small lie.

"I already told everybody I was Mary Poppins," Emma Lou said.

"Did I do something wrong, Mr. Mooney?" Clarissa asked.

"No, Clarissa, no one has done anything wrong."

Dorothy sat without moving. Although Mr. Mooney had not glanced in her direction, she knew that it was her part that was about to be changed.

"I'm worried about the end of the play. . . ."

Now everyone in the room looked at Dorothy. Her Tarzan yell was the end of the play.

"Let's see . . . let's see," Mr. Mooney said as if he were making a decision, although Dorothy knew the decision had already been made.

"I'm a little worried about the Tarzan yell." This was an understatement. He was extremely worried about the Tarzan yell.

"What's wrong with it?" Dorothy asked.

"Nothing's wrong with it."

"I thought it was good," Dwayne surprised himself by saying.

"Oh, it was, and"—Mr. Mooney swallowed—"it was getting better and better."

"Then what's wrong?" Dorothy asked.

"I'm not doing a very good job of explaining it, but I think, for the good of the production, it would be best if—well, I mean, what I've worked out is this. Clarissa will say her usual line, that some characters are recognized just by their sound. And you will say this."

He handed Dorothy a slip of paper. She stared at it in disbelief. Her mouth dropped open.

"Go ahead, Clarissa. Let's see how this will work."

With a rustle of paper Clarissa found the correct page in her script. She said, "Some characters on the pages we have found can be known just by their sound."

There was a silence. Everyone in the room looked at Dorothy. Dorothy looked at the slip of paper in her hand.

"Read it, please," Mr. Mooney said.

Dorothy shook her head.

"Read it!" This was a command.

With a voice that quivered, Dorothy read, "Th-th-that's all, folks."

There was a shocked silence, even more pronounced than the silences that followed her Tarzan yells.

Finally Dorothy said, "But Mr. Mooney, it's not a literary character who says that. It's a cartoon character."

"Porky Pig," someone in the back of the room offered.

"He's also in comic books," Clarissa said to be helpful. "So maybe that makes him a literary character."

"Gang," Mr. Mooney said, and he had a look on his face that they had seen a few times before and had hoped never to see again. "Who is the boss of this room?"

"You are!" Everyone but Dorothy answered.

"And as boss of the room, does that make me

responsible for everything that happens in this room?"

"Yes!"

He spoke more carefully this time so they would get the connection. "And does that make me responsible for what this room does together as a class?"

"Yes!"

"Dorothy, I didn't hear your voice."

"Yes."

"And since I am responsible for what this room does as a class, does that include a play we put on in the school auditorium?"

"Yes!"

"And if I feel that a line in the play must be changed, then isn't it my duty to change that line?"

"Yes!"

"And so what will your line be in the new version of the play, Dorothy?"

"Th-th-that's all, folks."

Fifteen / The Yell of Her Life

"I think it's cruddy."

Dorothy spun around. She was walking home, so intent on her own thoughts that she had not been aware that Dwayne had gotten off the bus at her stop.

Not only had he gotten off, but he had followed her.

"I think it's really cruddy," Dwayne said.

"What?"

"Taking your Tarzan yell out of the play. Your yell—" He paused.

"Yes?" she said defensively. She didn't think Dwayne would have anything nice to say about her yell.

"Well, it was the best part of the play."

"Oh?"

"It was the only good thing in the play."

"Oh?"

Dorothy wished she could think of something else to say, but she was too surprised.

"All the rest of the play—well, it was just the ordinary school play, something for parents. But then your yell somehow made it different, something that really, I don't know, meant something.

"When I heard Clarissa give your introduction, I realized I was really looking forward to your yell. I liked to hear it for some reason. And when you said, 'Th-th-that's all, folks,' I felt let down."

"Do you mean that?"

"I wouldn't have said it if I didn't mean it."

"Because I appreciate it."

"Well, I just wanted to let you know that I think Mr. Mooney made a mistake."

"I do too."

Dorothy grinned for the first time since Mr. Mooney had handed her that humiliating slip of paper.

"But there's one thing about mistakes," she said.

"What's that?"

"Sometimes they can be corrected."

He stared at her, thinking of what she had just

said. "You mean you're not going to do the Porky Pig thing?"

"That's right."

"You're going to do the Tarzan yell?"

"You got it." She grinned. "Not only am I going to do the Tarzan yell, but it's going to be the Tarzan yell of my life."

"That I've got to hear."

"You will."

Sixteen / The Big Top

"Popcorn! Cotton candy! Hot dogs! Right this way!"

"Get your souvenir programs! Buy 'em while they last!"

"Hot roasted peanuts! Cotton candy! The show is about to begin! Get your hot roasted peanuts! Cotton candy!"

Behind the big tent the elephants were eating hay. The elephant tender was brushing the bright-colored drapes that adorned their backs.

The ringmaster watched the elephants. He said to the trainer, "The animals seem to be all right tonight."

The elephant trainer nodded. "I don't know what got into them the other afternoon."

"And the night before that," the ringmaster reminded him. "I'll be glad when we leave this town. Things don't feel right."

"In all my years with elephants, I never saw anything like it. It was scary the way they all got restless at the same time, like they heard something from far off they wanted to follow. What could be calling them in a town like this?"

"Beats me."

Performers were moving in and out of their trailers, putting on their costumes for the performance. Clowns mingled with acrobats and daredevil motorcyclists.

The Alvarez sisters calmed their doves in Spanish, and the bear trainer told Snookums in Russian not to worry. But the performers seemed nervous too, as if they had caught the animals' anxiety.

The ringmaster picked up his whistle and blew a blast that got everyone's attention.

"Fifteen minutes," he said.

Performers and workers began moving a little faster, getting ready for the show.

The spectators had bought their tickets and were piling into the tent now, finding their seats. There was an air of expectation, of the wonderful feeling that what they were about to see was real, no magic, no tricks of the TV camera, but real risk-your-life tricks.

The smell of the circus filled their senses—the ripe horse sweat, the fresh sawdust, the oily smell of the waterproofed canvas overhead.

The ringmaster blew his whistle again. "Ten minutes!" The activity behind the big top increased. Then, "Five minutes!" and the performers and animals lined up for the big walk-around that opened the show.

Leading off were the horses, mounted by riders in red, white, and blue, their American flags held high. Uncle Sam on stilts followed.

After that a girl in a silky costume rode the largest elephant. There were clowns, the Alvarez sisters with doves on their outstretched arms, the zebras, the camel, the Astros, who rode motorcycles on high wires, and Chinese acrobats. Last were the other elephants in bespangled blankets, moving trunk to tail, with attendants alongside.

The ringmaster glanced back. Everyone was in place. The trainers had tailed up the elephants. Still . . .

The ringmaster shook his head. He couldn't get rid of the feeling that tonight's performance was somehow doomed. And there was nothing he could do about it.

Squaring his shoulders, the ringmaster went inside the tent. He stepped into the center ring and picked up his microphone. A spotlight shone on him, and the crowd grew quiet at the sight of him in his bright-red jacket, black silk top hat, white riding breeches, and black shiny boots.

"Ladies and gentlemen," he said, "and children of all ages, welcome to the one hundred and thirtieth edition of the Rogers Brothers Circus!"

The time was seven thirty.

The time was seven thirty.

The place was the school auditorium.

"That concludes our business meeting," the principal was saying. "And now, parents, teachers, students, and guests, we have a special treat. Mr. Herb Mooney's class has prepared a play entitled 'Literary Characters We Love and Hope You Do Too.' Mr. Mooney, I'll turn the program over to you."

Mr. Mooney stepped out from behind the curtain and said modestly, "This is really the kids' show." On that cue the class filed onstage and got in line. Then Mr. Mooney said, "Clarissa!"

"Welcome to our show," Clarissa said, obviously pleased with her stage voice. "Mr. Mooney's class is proud to present a revue of famous characters from the books we have come to love.

"Throughout history there have been characters that seem to walk off the page. Why, here's one now."

Dwayne made his way to the front of the stage. He was even more nervous than the rest of the class, because he knew how the play was going to end.

He paused, and Clarissa rolled her eyes and hissed, "These hands, these feet—"

"Oh, yeah," said Dwayne. "These hands, these feet, this chin, they are not mine. My designer label reads Frankenstein."

He had intended to say, "Frrrrankenstein," but in his nervousness, he forgot. He felt lucky he didn't forget to step back into line. Anyway, he figured no one—not even his parents—would remember his part in this pitiful play, not after Dorothy's Tarzan.

There was applause from Dwayne's parents, and Dorothy's mother took that moment to lean over and say to her husband, "I ought to feel relieved. I know Dorothy's got a new part to say."

"Then act relieved."

"I'm trying to, but you know Dorothy. She's got a mind of her own. She—"

Mary Poppins' mother said, "Shhh." Her daughter had just stepped to center stage and was opening her umbrella. For her this was the good part.

In the wings Mr. Mooney said to himself, "It's going well." And then he added the thought that troubled him like a bad tooth: If only Dorothy doesn't . . .

The play continued. The actors said their lines perfectly, and the play was now coming to a successful end.

Some of the parents in the audience had been counting, and now only Dorothy was left to say her lines.

Clarissa said, "Some characters on the pages we have found can be known just by their sound."

"This is it! This is it!" Dorothy's mom whispered. She reached over and took her husband's hand for luck.

She watched as Dorothy stepped forward. Her own mouth formed the words she so wanted her daughter to say. "Th-th-that's all, folks."

In the wings Mr. Mooney's mouth silently formed the same words. But it didn't appear to either of them that Dorothy's mouth was doing the same.

Dorothy took another step forward. Her hands went to her chest. Her mother saw that they were fists.

"Oh, no. Here we go."

She watched as Dorothy took in a deep breath. She could see from the look on her daughter's face that she smelled the lushness of tropical trees, that she heard native drums, that she was in the jungle.

And then Dorothy opened her mouth.

AHHHHHHH-
AHH-AHH-AAHH-
AHHHHH-AHH-
AHH-AHH-
AHHHHHHHHH

There was absolute silence. No one in the auditorium moved or spoke.

Dorothy stood in the center of the stage with her fists at her chest. She had a wild look on her face, as if she were still in the jungle. The rest of the people didn't know exactly where they were, because for a moment they, too, had been where the wild things are.

The silence was broken by a little boy in the front row. "Mama, I wet my pants."

nineteen / Lions and Tigers and Bears, Oh, My!

After the revelation of the kid who'd wet his pants, the audience began a general uneasy shifting in their seats. Perhaps the kid had not been the only one.

Finally Mr. Mooney stepped out from behind the curtain. His expression said that he did not want to be doing this. He didn't know what to say. The only thing he could think of was "Th-th-that's all, folks," and that wouldn't be appropriate.

Mr. Mooney never got the chance to speak, because there was a noise outside the auditorium that caught everyone's attention. The noise was even more startling than the Tarzan yell.

The noise . . . that noise . . . The audience lifted their heads. Mr. Mooney peered at the back of the auditorium. What was it?

The noise was something the audience had never heard before, that was for sure. It was the sound that came from the football stadium sometimes—but different; the sound an earthquake might make when tearing the earth apart, though none of them had heard an earthquake so they couldn't be sure; the sound of Niagara Falls, jet planes, a hurricane. It was all those sounds rolled into one.

And then one man who saw a lot of western movies recognized the sound.

"Stampede!"

At once the audience turned to the back of the auditorium. They saw the open doors. Everybody wished someone would get up and shut those doors, but nobody could move. It was as if they were stuck to their seats.

"Don't panic," Mr. Mooney advised.

But it wasn't the audience who was in a panic—it was the animals that began to pour through the open doors of the auditorium.

The auditorium became filled with animals—horses, a zebra with a poodle on its back, a donkey, a pygmy hippo, ponies with monkey jockeys, performing dogs, and a baby elephant.

The larger elephants, two of them trying to get through the doors at the same time, got stuck, performing the merciful act of keeping any other animals out. Still, this didn't stop them from throwing back their heads and trumpeting.

There was room over the elephants' heads for the trained doves, and they flew in, cooing and flapping their wings in a wide circle.

The ringmaster arrived, couldn't get through the doors, and ran around to a side entrance. He appeared onstage looking in a dazed fashion at the frightened and confused animals in the aisles of the auditorium.

"What's happened? What's happened?"

Mr. Mooney tried to explain, over the thundering cries of animals, that one of his students had given this yell and—

"Where are the trainers? Somebody get the trainers in here. We have got to get these animals back to the circus."

Clarissa stepped up to the ringmaster. "She did it." She pointed to Dorothy.

"What?"

"She did it. You don't need the trainers. She can just go over to your circus and give her stupid yell and get your animals back."

"Which girl? Where?"

Clarissa again pointed to Dorothy.

"That girl!"

Twenty / That Girl

Dorothy stood in the center ring of the circus. She was pale, shaken. The whole big top was filled with people looking at her, waiting.

Her mother, her father, and the ringmaster were beside her. Dwayne was too. She had insisted on that. She had surprised and pleased him by saying, "He's my friend, Mom."

"Go ahead," said her mother. "Give your yell."

Dorothy swallowed.

"Go ahead, Dorothy," she urged, louder this time. "Everyone is waiting."

"I know."

"Just give her a minute," Dwayne said.

Dorothy gave him a look of thanks. She could see

that her mom was watching sixty seconds tick off on her watch.

"A minute's up. Go ahead, Dorothy."

"I don't think I can."

"Of course you can," her mother said. "You've been doing this yell for four days now. You've given me headaches and upset animals all over creation and—"

Her father interrupted. "Why can't you, Dorothy?"

"I don't know if I can explain it, Dad, but always before, well, the yell was an expression, I don't know, of freedom, a celebration of freedom, and that's why the animals came, because they sensed that's what it was. If I gave the yell now, it would be the opposite; it would be taking their freedom away."

"But Dorothy," her dad said, "because of your yell, the animals did get to run free. It was one of the wildest, happiest stampedes I ever saw in my life."

"Or ever hope to see," her mom added under her breath."

"Well, yeah," her dad admitted.

"But now, Dorothy," he went on, "now they've done their thing, and you know what they're doing now, don't you?"

"No."

"They're just standing around out in front of the auditorium looking at each other. The doves are sitting up in the trees. Somebody said they looked dazed. They don't know what to do with themselves."

"They don't?"

"No, and somehow, some way, they're going to have to get back here. These animals have never lived outside the circus, Dorothy. The circus is the only home they know. They wouldn't survive on their own. If you really can't do it, then they'll have to figure something else out. But think of this. Your yell would give the animals one more wild, happy stampede before they come back home."

"Give me a minute." Dorothy drew in a breath. It wasn't the jungle she smelled; it was ripe horse sweat, hay mixed with pungent elephant dung, fresh sawdust, and the oily canvas overhead.

"It's not coming."

"Try, Dorothy."

"I am trying."

Dorothy tried hard to think of the jungle, to get a whiff of the lush tropical trees, to hear the jungle drums.

She opened her mouth. Nothing.

From beside her, Dwayne said, "Maybe I could do it."

Dorothy turned to him in astonishment. "You?"

"Yes, me. Why not? I've seen how you do it."

"It's not a matter of seeing how I do it. It's in the mind, Dwayne."

"Well, maybe you won't believe it, but I've got one of those too." His tone changed, softened. "If you'd help me, I'm sure I could do it."

"Dwayne, first you have to smell the jungle."

"I do smell it. I smell more jungle than I ever smelled in my life."

"You're smelling the circus."

"But if I think it's the jungle, wouldn't that be the same thing? Let me try, all right?"

Dwayne stepped back—he didn't want to blow them all away. He took a deep breath. He actually did smell the jungle. He opened his mouth.

AHHHHHH-AHH-AHH-AAHH-AHHHHH-AHH-AHH-AHH-AHHHHHHHHHHHH!

"That was pitiful."

"It was just my first try. I understand how to do it now. Listen:

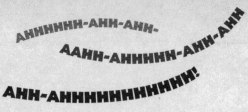

AHHHHHH-AHH-AHH-
AAHH-AHHHHH-AHH-AHH
AHH-AHHHHHHHHHHH!

That was better, wasn't it?"

"It was louder, but I don't see any animals yet."

"I can do it, I tell you, I can do it!"

"Kids," the ringmaster said, "if you can't get the animals, we need to move."

"I can do it. I can!" He stepped back for another try.

AHHHHHH-AHH-AHH-AAHH
AHHHHH-AHH-AHH-AHH-
AHHHHHHHHHHHHH!

"Not like that!" Dorothy yelled, "Not like that! Like this!"

AHHHH

Twenty-one / Home

Everyone stood in place, head high, listening. Even Uncle Sam on stilts, towering over them all, looked skyward.

Then they heard it—the sound that came from stadiums, earthquakes, Niagara Falls, jet planes, hurricanes, and stampedes. This time they knew which one it was.

The Alvarez sisters rushed to the opening in the tent to call encouragement to their trained doves. "Come to Mama," they cried, arms outstretched.

Their cries were joined by those of a huge man in a cossack cloak calling for his bear. "Snookums! Snookums!"

"Out of the way, everyone!" the ringmaster called. "They're coming!"

Dorothy moved to the bleachers with her parents and Dwayne.

The horses were first, with the zebra close behind. Then came the doves, circling the arena and landing on their trainers' outstretched arms.

"Oh, the bear!" Dorothy said to Dwayne. "I didn't even know there was a bear, did you?"

"I knew there was a bear," Dwayne said. "I smelled him."

The Russian brown bear came into the circus tent, and his huge trainer embraced him. "Snookums, Snookums, I tink I lose you! I tink I never see you no more." Tears rolled down the trainer's cheeks.

The elephant trainer's triumphant cries—"Jules! Fanny! Queen! Lou! Shug!"—rose above the other shouts as, one by one, the elephants padded together into the arena. Their huge feet hit the earth with such force that Dorothy felt the bleachers tremble beneath her.

When the last of the animals, the pygmy hippo, had returned, Dwayne turned to Dorothy and said, "Well, you did it. You got them back."

Dorothy nodded.

But as she watched the scene around her, she understood that she hadn't gotten the animals back alone. She had merely shown them the way.

Twenty-two / The Parade

Once again the ringmaster stood in the spotlight. Once again he lifted the microphone.

"Ladies and gentlemen," he said. His voice boomed over the loudspeaker. "And children of all ages, welcome to the one hundred and thirtieth edition of the Rogers Brothers Circus!"

The three-piece band struck up a bright march, and the parade began.

Dorothy and Dwayne sat in the front row, honored guests of the circus. After her last Tarzan yell Dorothy had been ready to go home, but her parents and the ringmaster and Dwayne had kept after her, begging her to stay. "If it weren't for you," Dwayne had said, "there wouldn't be a circus." So here she was.

The first performers in the parade were the

horseback riders in red, white, and blue outfits, holding American flags. As the horses pranced by, their heads nodding, Dorothy began to realize she would actually enjoy herself. She recognized these horses—they had been among the first to burst into the auditorium.

And the camel! She would never forget how proud of himself he had been to be in the auditorium. And the zebra with a dog on his back. The Alvarez sisters with their doves, the roller-skating Snookums—she felt they were part of her. Well, for a while they actually had been.

"You're smiling. What are you thinking about?" Dwayne asked.

"Just that I'm enjoying myself."

"Me too."

"But," she went on, "I was also thinking that if we have another play, I am not going to be in it."

"Why? You were the best one!"

"Well, thanks, but I get sort of—I guess you could say carried away."

"That's what makes you a good actress."

"You did good too."

Three days ago, when she'd sent that note to him, *Me Tarzan, you Dwayne*; even two days ago, when he had sent her that *What was that last night? One of your apes?*—she had had no idea she'd be sitting beside him at a circus, listening to him saying nice things about her, and saying nice things back.

"Anyway," Dwayne said, "I don't think Mr. Mooney will be having a play anytime soon. I heard him say, 'That's all, folks,' and it did not sound like a line from a cartoon."

"That's what I said about my Tarzan yells."

"You aren't going to do any more?"

"No! I don't think I could even if I wanted to."

"If Mr. Mooney changed his mind and we did another play—"

"I won't!"

"I know, but I'm curious. If we did another play, what would you want to be?"

"Oh, well, when I was trying to get you to give the Tarzan yell, I was reminded of a scene in *Peter Pan* where Peter's trying to get the kids to crow like a rooster, and they keep getting a little louder and a little louder and finally they get it."

"But I didn't get it."

"You might have. Anyway, if we did another play—which I absolutely will not be in—I'd probably want to be Peter Pan. Of course, I don't know whether I could actually fly or not."

Dwayne looked at her with admiration. "I bet you could," he said.

"Maybe. Oh, look, here come the elephants!"